For the Rutkowski Farmers: Paul, Kathleen, and Asa

Balzer + Bray is an imprint of HarperCollins Publishers.

Oink-a-Doodle-Moo
Copyright © 2012 by Jef Czekaj
All rights reserved. Manufactured in China. No part of this book may be used or reproduced in any manner
whatsoever without written permission except in the case of brief quotations embodied in critical articles
and reviews. For information address HarperCollins Children's Books, a division of HarperCollins Publishers,
10 East 53rd Street, New York, NY 10022. www.harpercollinschildrens.com.

Library of Congress Cataloging-in-Publication Data
Czekaj, Jef.
  Oink-a-doodle-moo / Jef Czekaj. — 1st ed.
    p. cm.
  Summary: In a barnyard, a pig whispers into a rooster's ear, starting a game of "telephone" that goes
horribly awry.
  ISBN 978-0-06-206011-2 (trade bdg.)
  [1. Animal sounds—Fiction. 2. Domestic animals—Fiction. 3. Humorous stories.] I. Title.
PZ7.C9987Oi 2012   2011010065
[E]—dc22   CIP
                                                                    AC

Typography by Dana Fritts
12 13 14 15 16 SCP 10 9 8 7 6 5 4 3 2 1

❖ First Edition

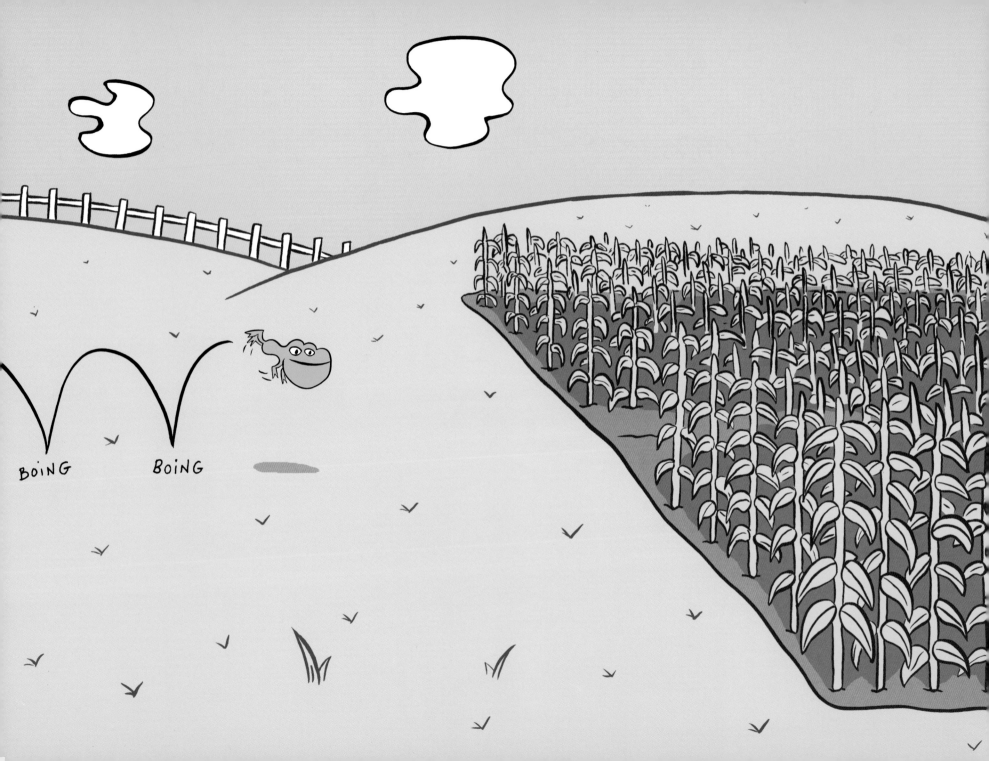

Pass it on.

Pass it on.

we'll just start over!

To the memory of my dear Marijane. — R.E.A.

With love to my husband, Tom, whose compassion, intelligence and
  courage have made our lives interesting, and whose humor has made
  our lives fun.— S.L.

Text copyright © 1994 by Richard E. Albert.
Illustrations copyright © 1994 by Sylvia Long.
All rights reserved.
Book design by Laura Lovett
Printed in China

Library of Congress Cataloging in Publication Data
Albert, Richard E. , 1909-
        Alejandro's gift/ by Richard E. Albert; illustrated by Sylvia Long.
        p. cm.
Summary: Lonely in his house beside a road in the desert, Alejandro builds an oasis
to attract the many animals around him.
ISBN: 0-8118-1342-8 (pb)
ISBN: 0-8118-0436-4 (hc)
[1. Desert animals—Fiction.] I. Long, Sylvia, ill. II. Title.
PZ7.A32137A1   1994
[E]—dc20   93-30199
                                                   CIP
                                                   AC

Distributed in Canada by Raincoast Books
8680 Cambie Street
Vancouver, B.C. V6P 6M9

Distributed in Australia and New Zealand by CIS•Cardigan Street
245-249 Cardigan Street, Carlton 3053 Australia

10 9 8 7 6 5 4 3

Chronicle Books
275 Fifth Street
San Francisco, CA 94103

ALEJANDRO'S GIFT

BY RICHARD E. ALBERT

ILLUSTRATED BY SYLVIA LONG

chronicle books

SAN FRANCISCO

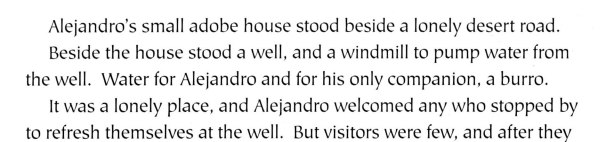

Alejandro's small adobe house stood beside a lonely desert road.
Beside the house stood a well, and a windmill to pump water from the well. Water for Alejandro and for his only companion, a burro.
It was a lonely place, and Alejandro welcomed any who stopped by to refresh themselves at the well. But visitors were few, and after they left, Alejandro felt lonelier than before.

To more easily endure the lonely hours, Alejandro planted a garden.
A garden filled with carrots, beans, and large brown onions.
Tomatoes and corn.
Melons, squash, and small red peppers.
Most mornings found Alejandro tending the garden, watching it grow. These were times he cherished, and he often stayed for hours, working until driven indoors by the desert heat.
The days went by, one after another with little change, until one morning when there was an unexpected visitor. This visitor came not from the desert road, but from the desert itself.

A ground squirrel crept from the underbrush. Moving warily over the sand, it hesitated and looked around. Alejandro paused, keeping very quiet as the squirrel approached the garden. It ran up to one of the furrows, drank its fill of water, and scampered away. After it left, Alejandro realized that for those few moments his loneliness had been all but forgotten.

And because he felt less lonely, Alejandro found himself hoping the squirrel would come again.

The squirrel did come again, from time to time bringing along small friends.

Wood rats and pocket gophers.

Jackrabbits, kangaroo rats, pocket mice.

Birds, too, became aware of Alejandro's garden.

Roadrunners, gila woodpeckers, thrashers.

Cactus wrens, sage sparrows, mourning doves, and others came in the evening to perch on the branches of a mesquite bush, or to rest on the arms of a lone saguaro, before dropping down for a quick drink before nightfall.

Occasionally, even an old desert tortoise could be seen plodding toward the garden.

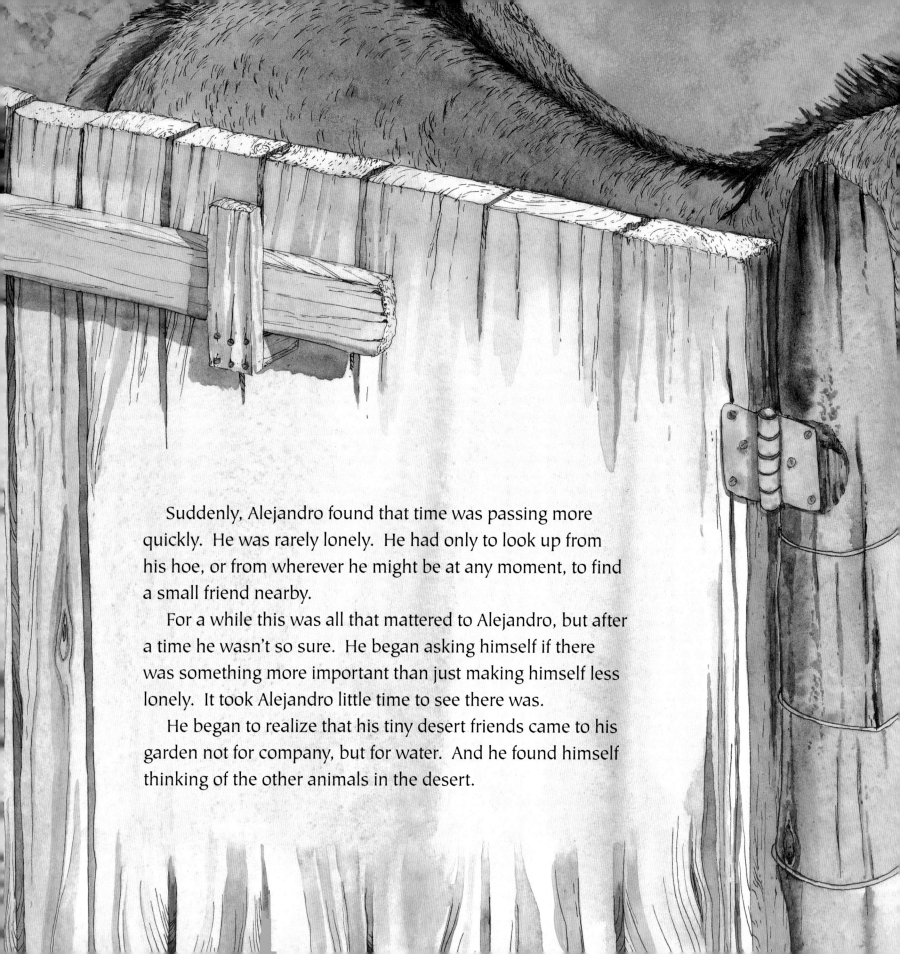

Suddenly, Alejandro found that time was passing more quickly. He was rarely lonely. He had only to look up from his hoe, or from wherever he might be at any moment, to find a small friend nearby.

For a while this was all that mattered to Alejandro, but after a time he wasn't so sure. He began asking himself if there was something more important than just making himself less lonely. It took Alejandro little time to see there was.

He began to realize that his tiny desert friends came to his garden not for company, but for water. And he found himself thinking of the other animals in the desert.

Animals like the coyote and the desert gray fox.

The bobcats, the skunks, the badgers, the long-nosed coatis.

The peccaries, sometimes called *javelinas*, the short-tempered wild pigs of the desert.

The antlered mule deer, the does, and the fawns.

Finding enough water was not a problem. With his windmill and well, Alejandro could supply ample water for any and all. Getting it to those who needed it was something else.

The something else, Alejandro decided, was a desert water hole.

Without delay, Alejandro started digging. It was tiring work, taking many days in the hot desert sun. But the thought of giving water to so many thirsty desert dwellers more than made up for the drudgery. And when it was filled, Alejandro was pleased with the gift he had made for his desert friends.

There was good reason to suppose it would take time for the larger animals to discover their new source of water, so Alejandro was patient. He went about as usual, feeding his burro, tending the garden, and doing countless other chores.

Days passed and nothing happened. Still, Alejandro was confident. But the days turned to weeks, and it was still quiet at the water hole. Why, Alejandro wondered, weren't they coming? What could he have done wrong?

The absence of the desert folk might have remained a mystery had Alejandro not come out of the house one morning when a skunk was in the clearing beyond the water hole. Seeing Alejandro, the skunk darted to safety in the underbrush.

It suddenly became very clear why Alejandro's gift was being shunned.

Alejandro couldn't believe he had been so thoughtless, but what was important now was to put things right as quickly as possible.

Water hole number two was built far from the house and screened
by heavy desert growth. When it was filled and ready, Alejandro waited
with mixed emotions. He was hopeful, yet he couldn't forget what had
happened the first time.

As it turned out, he was not disappointed.

The animals of the desert did come, each as it made its own discovery. Because the water hole was now sheltered from the small adobe house and the desert road, the animals were no longer fearful. And although Alejandro could not see through the desert growth surrounding the water hole, he had ways of knowing it was no longer being shunned.

By the twitter of birds gathering in the dusk.

By the rustling of mesquite in the quiet desert evening telling of the approach of a coyote, a badger, or maybe a desert fox.

By the soft hoofbeats of a mule deer, or the unmistakable sound of a herd of peccaries charging toward the water hole.

And in these moments when Alejandro sat quietly listening
to the sounds of his desert neighbors, he knew that the gift was
not so much a gift that he had given, but a gift he had received.

The Southwestern region of the United States is made up of Colorado, Arizona, New Mexico, and Utah. A variety of wildlife can be found in its varied habitats. The following glossary lists some of the animals and plants shown in this book.

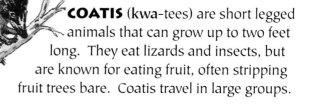

COATIS (kwa-tees) are short legged animals that can grow up to two feet long. They eat lizards and insects, but are known for eating fruit, often stripping fruit trees bare. Coatis travel in large groups.

The **ARIZONA POCKET MOUSE** eats many kinds of seeds and can hibernate when food cannot be found.

The **COLLARED PECCARY** (peck-a-ree) resembles a wild pig but has a snout that points upwards. It eats cacti—especially prickly pear, which it devours spines and all. During the midday heat, peccaries often sleep in hollows in the ground.

BADGERS have distinctive black-and-white "masks" on their faces. They live in family groups in underground burrows. Few animals will attack the badger because of its fierce temperament.

The **BLACK-TAILED JACK-RABBIT** has very large ears, which help keep it cool in hot weather. It also has very large feet, which help it run quickly.

COSTA'S HUMMINGBIRD is a purple-throated hummingbird no more than 3½ inches long. As it hovers over flowers, its wings beat so fast they make a humming sound. Hummingbirds are the only birds that can hover.

BOBCATS get their name from their stubby "bobbed" tail. They are found only in North America, where they are the most common wildcat. They eat small mammals, such as rabbits, mice, and squirrels. The bobcat barks hoarsely when threatened.

COYOTES can run as fast as 40 miles per hour and leap as far as 14 feet. They run with their tails down, unlike wolves, which run with their tails straight behind them.

The **CURVE-BILLED THRASHER** is about the size of a robin. It has a long, curved bill and red eyes. It lives in cactus deserts and eats insects.

BOTTA'S POCKET GOPHER spends most of its time in underground burrows, some of which can be as long as 150 feet. Botta's Pocket Gophers live by themselves, often fighting other gophers they meet.

The **DESERT TORTOISE** stores water in a pouch beneath its shell. It hibernates underground from October to March. Desert Tortoises can grow up to 15 inches long.

The **ELF OWL** is the smallest American owl and is no bigger than a sparrow. It lives in saguaro deserts and feeds on large insects.

The **CACTUS WREN** is the largest North American wren—growing up to 9 inches long. It lives in nests in clumps of mesquite on desert hillsides.

GAMBEL'S QUAIL lives in desert thickets. This bird has a loud, cackling call, and a large teardrop-shaped feather on its head.

The **GILA WOODPECKER** nests in holes in giant saguaro cacti. Its feathers are patterned in black and white stripes. Males have a small red cap, while females and young birds have plain brown heads.

The **GRAY FOX** is mostly active at night, but can sometimes be seen during the day looking for food. They are the only canids (the family of wolves, foxes, coyote, and dogs) that can climb, and they often rest in trees.

The **GREATER ROADRUNNER** is a tall bird (20 to 24 inches) that rarely flies, running instead on strong feet. It eats a wide variety of small animals, including snakes, lizards, and scorpions.

HARRIS'S ANTELOPE SQUIRREL lives in low deserts. Its pale coloring helps it blend with the environment. Antelope Squirrels get most of the water they need from the food they eat.

MERRIAM'S KANGAROO RAT is the smallest kangaroo rat in the United States. It lives in scrublands, feeding mostly on the seeds of mesquite and other desert plants.

MESQUITE (mess-keet) is a spiny tree that grows in large thickets in the Southwest and Mexico.

The **MOURNING DOVE**'s name comes from its melancholy cooing, which is its mating call. Mourning doves can be found all over North America.

MULE DEER have large ears and are one of the most common animals of the desert. Their diet consists of grasses, twigs, and cactus fruits. Mule Deer can run up to 35 miles an hour, and can jump as far as 25 feet.

The **PHAINOPEPLA** (fay-no-pep-la) is a tropical bird with an elegant crest on its head. It eats mistletoe berries and insects, which it snatches right out of the air.

SAGE SPARROWS are small brown birds with white eye rings. They are found in dry foothills and sagebrush.

The **SAGUARO** (sah-gwar-oh) is a cactus that can grow up to 60 feet tall. It provides fruit for many desert creatures, and bears white flowers.

The **WHITE-THROATED WOOD RAT** usually lives in the base of a cactus, and it uses the cactus needles to hide the entrance to its home.